To the Little Yellow Leaf in all of us
and to the Little Scarlet Leaves
that help us find our courage

Also, as always, to Thea, my most excellent editor,
and with great appreciation to MM, LF, and VAD

The Little Yellow Leaf. Copyright © 2008 by Carin Berger. All rights reserved. Manufactured in China.
www.harpercollinschildrens.com. Collages were used to prepare the full-color art. The text type is 20-point Bernhard
Modern. Library of Congress Cataloging-in-Publication Data. Berger, Carin. The little yellow leaf / by Carin Berger.
p. cm. "Greenwillow Books." Summary: A yellow leaf is not ready to fall from the tree when autumn comes, but finally,
after finding another leaf still on the tree, the two let go together. ISBN 978-0-06-145223-9 (trade bdg.)
ISBN 978-0-06-145224-6 (lib. bdg.) [1. Leaves—Fiction.] I. Title. PZ7.B45134Li 2008 [E]—dc22 2007039191
First Edition 10 9 8 7 6 5 4 3 2 1
Greenwillow Books

The Little Yellow Leaf

Carin Berger

Greenwillow Books
An Imprint of HarperCollins Publishers

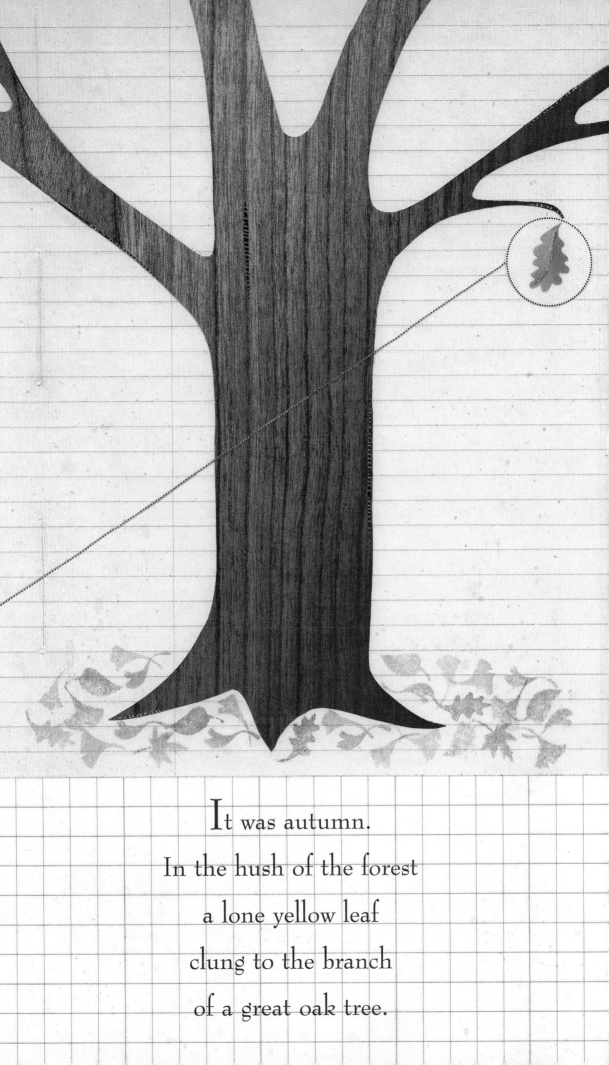

It was autumn.

In the hush of the forest

a lone yellow leaf

clung to the branch

of a great oak tree.

I'm not ready yet, thought the Little Yellow Leaf as

a riot of fiery leaves chased and swirled round the tree.

Not yet, thought the Little Yellow Leaf . . .

as the afternoon sun

beckoned and teased.

Not ready, thought
the Little Yellow Leaf
as apples grew musky,
pumpkins heavy,
and flocks of geese
took wing.

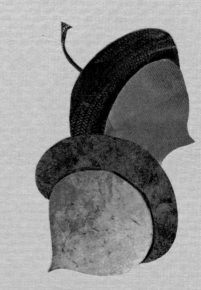

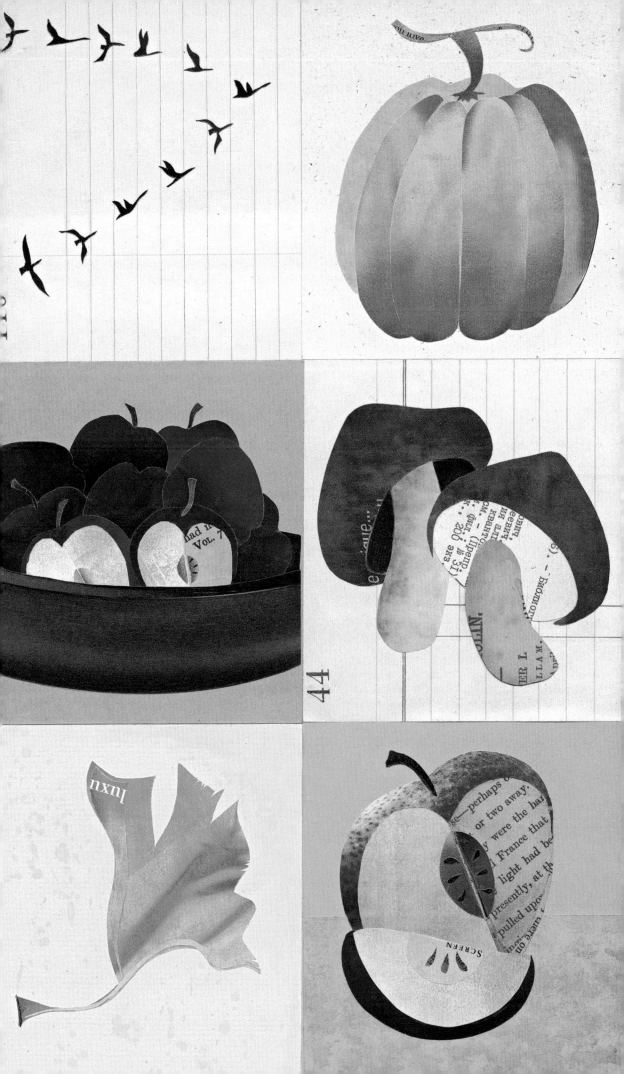

Still not,

he thought

as the other leaves gathered

into great heaps,

crackly dry,

where children

played.

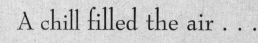
A chill filled the air . . .

Not ready,

thought the Little Yellow Leaf

as a heavy harvest moon

bloomed

amber

in the starry sky.

Not yet, not yet, not yet.

Through the long night,
snow flurried
and the Little Yellow Leaf
held fast
to the great oak tree.

Days passed by

and still the Little Yellow Leaf

held tight.

Alone.

He searched the bare, bare branches

covered only with

a shimmer of snow.

Alone.

And then . . . and then, high up on an icy branch, ← a scarlet flash. One more leaf holding tight.

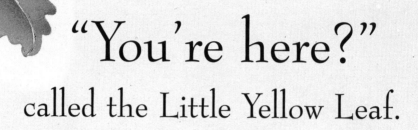

"You're here?"

called the Little Yellow Leaf.

"I am,"

said the Little Scarlet Leaf.

"Like me!"

said the Little Yellow Leaf.

Neither spoke. Finally . . .

"Will you?"
asked the Little Scarlet Leaf.

"I will!"
said the Little Yellow Leaf.

And one, two, three, they let go and soared.

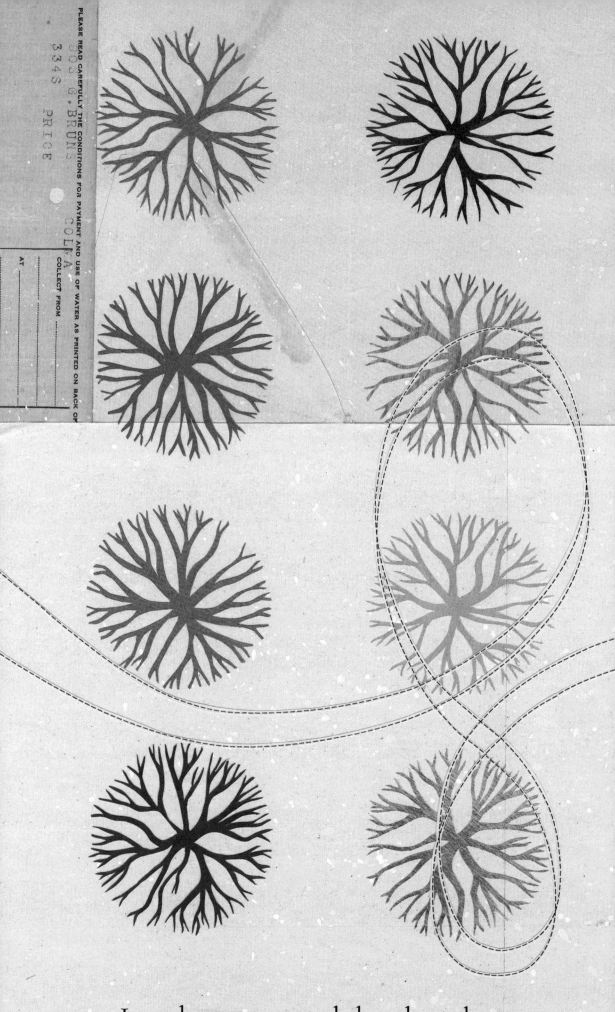

Into the waiting wind they danced . . .

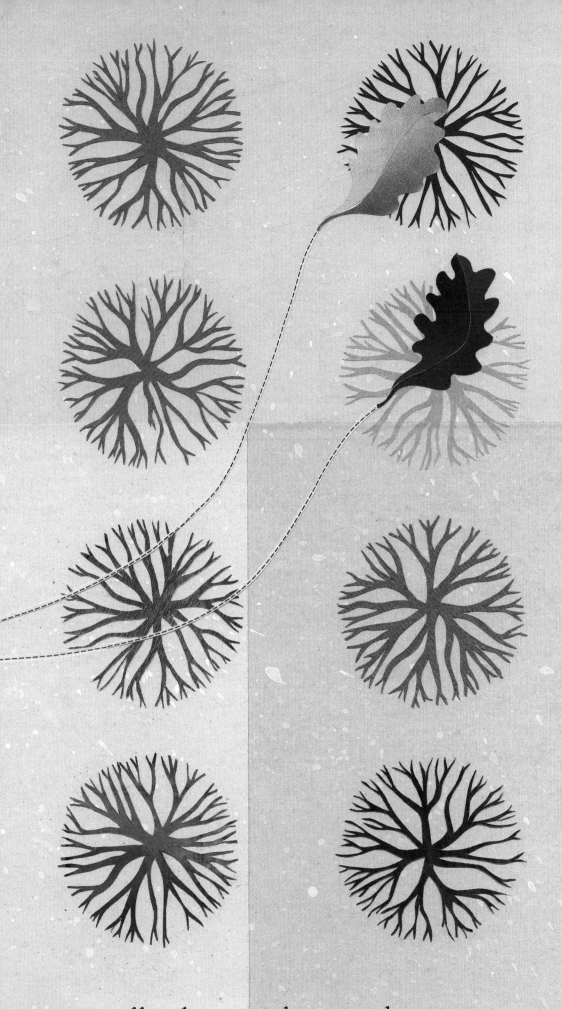

off and away and away and away.

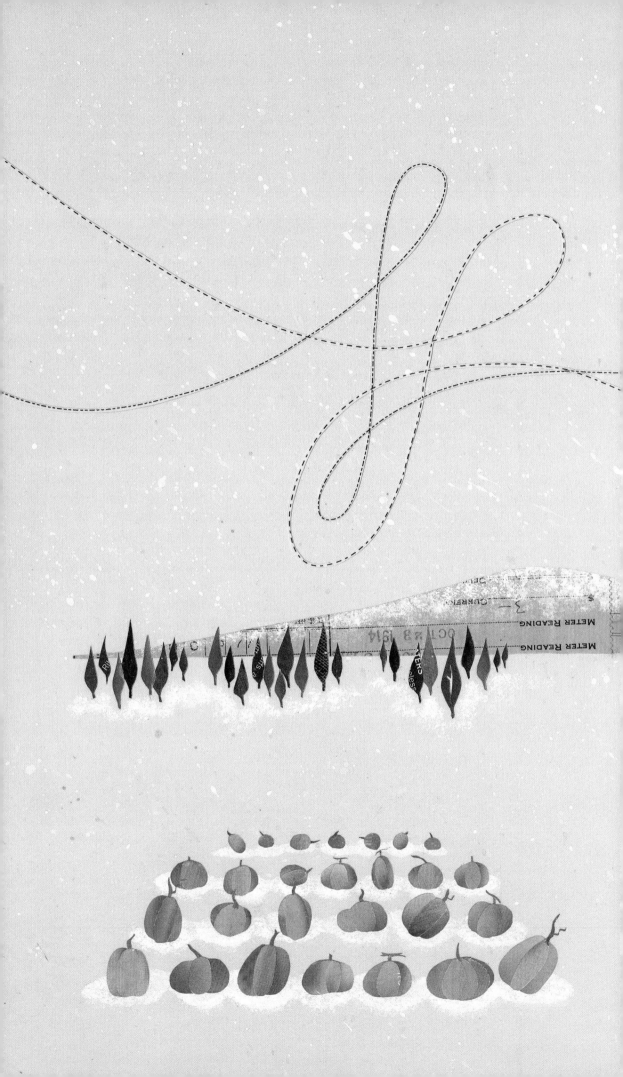

Together.

DATE DUE

PERMA-BOUND